Feeling
SCARED!

Published in North America by Free Spirit Publishing Inc., Minneapolis, Minnesota, 2017

Library of Congress Cataloging-in-Publication Data
Names: Barnham, Kay, author. | Gordon, Mike, 1948 March 16– illustrator.
Title: Feeling scared! / written by Kay Barnham ; illustrated by Mike Gordon.
Description: Minneapolis, Minnesota : Free Spirit Publishing Inc., 2017. | Series: Everyday Feelings
Identifiers: LCCN 2017008394 | ISBN 9781631982545 (hardcover) | ISBN 1631982540 (hardcover)
Subjects: LCSH: Fear in children—Juvenile literature. | Fear—Juvenile literature.
Classification: LCC BF723.F4 B37 2017 | DDC 155.4/1246—dc23 LC record available at https://lccn.loc.gov/2017008394

Free Spirit Publishing does not have control over or assume responsibility for author or third-party websites and their content.

Reading Level Grade 2; Interest Level Ages 5–9; Fountas & Pinnell Guided Reading Level L

10 9 8 7 6 5 4 3 2 1
Printed in China
H13660517

Free Spirit Publishing Inc.
6325 Sandburg Road, Suite 100
Minneapolis, MN 55427-3674
(612) 338-2068
help4kids@freespirit.com
www.freespirit.com

MIX
Paper from
responsible sources
FSC® C104740

First published in 2017 by Wayland, a division of Hachette Children's Books · London, UK, and Sydney, Australia
Text © Wayland 2017
Illustrations © Mike Gordon 2017

The rights of Kay Barnham to be identified as the author and Mike Gordon as the illustrator of this Work have been asserted in accordance with the Copyright, Designs and Patents Act, 1988.

Managing editor: Victoria Brooker
Creative design: Paul Cherrill

Feeling
SCARED!

Written by
Kay Barnham

Illustrated by
Mike Gordon

free spirit
PUBLISHING®

Something was wrong with Theo. Instead of kicking a ball around the playground, he was just leaning against a wall. When Diego got close, he could see that his best friend was actually trembling. "Are you sick?" asked Diego. "Should I take you to the school nurse?"

"Yes, *please*," groaned Theo.
"Then I won't have to do this stupid
talk in front of the class."

"What's the talk about?" asked Diego.

"Fast cars," said Theo.

"But you know so much about them," said Diego, surprised. "What's the problem?"

"I'm *scared*, okay?" snapped Theo.
"What if I make a mistake?

What if I get everything wrong?
What if everyone *laughs* at me?"

"I have an idea," Diego said. "Why don't you practice the talk in front of me?

I won't laugh if you get anything wrong. Then, when you do your talk, you'll know exactly what to say." "All right," said Theo. And he practiced in front of Diego.

Later, when Theo spoke in front of the class, his voice trembled at first. But his talk was great. "Phew!" he said to Diego. "That was easier than I thought. I feel great now. When can I do it again?"

That evening, there was a thunderstorm.

Lightning FLASHED.

Thunder BOOMED!

After a really loud roll of thunder,
Diego heard a small sob.
It was his sister, Rosie. She was hiding
behind the sofa, crying softly.

"Hey," said Diego, crouching down beside his sister, "do you know what thunder and lightning really are?"

Rosie shook her head.
"Not really," she whispered.
"I just know that I'm scared
and I want the storm
to STOP."

"When ice, hail, and rain in storm clouds rub together, they make a lot of electricity," Diego said. "Lightning is the flash that happens when the electricity jumps around."

"What about thunder?" asked Rosie.

"That's just the sound the lightning makes," said Diego. "We hear it later because light travels a lot faster than sound."

"It's not safe to stand under a tree or in
a big open space in a storm. But we're safe here.
Come on, let's watch it through the window."
Right then, a zigzag of lightning lit the sky.
"Wow!" gasped Rosie. "That's amazing!"

That weekend, Diego decided to visit his grandpa, who lived nearby. "Do you want to come?" he asked his friend Manish. "Grandpa always has lots of snacks," he added with a wink.

"But doesn't he have a dog, too?" asked Manish.
Diego nodded. "He's called Barney. He's COOL."

"Oh," said Manish,
his face falling.

"Don't you like dogs?"
asked Diego, puzzled.

"Not really,"
replied Manish.
"They scare
me a little."

"Some dogs can be loud and scary at first," said Diego. "But Barney's a great dog. He never growls and he doesn't bark much, either. Actually, the worst you can expect is a good licking."

"I'm still not sure," said Manish.

"Come on, I'll introduce you!" said Diego.

Diego's grandpa opened the door.
"Hi, boys!" he said, grinning widely. Barney
stood at his feet, wagging his tail furiously.
"Be warned, Manish," said Diego's grandpa.
"This is the goofiest dog
you will ever meet."

At first, Manish stayed away from Barney.
But after watching Diego play with him,
he bravely tried petting Barney.
"See?" said Diego. "Dogs aren't so bad
when you get to know them."
And Manish laughed as Barney licked his hand.

That night, it was Diego's turn to be
scared. He lay in bed thinking of the spooky movie
he'd seen that afternoon. In the movie, there
were monsters hiding under the bed.
What if monsters were hiding under *his* bed?

"ARRRGHHHH!"

whispered Diego
in a very small
voice, in case
the monsters
heard him.

And even though moonlight shone outside,
it was *so* dark in Diego's bedroom.
Shadows of ogres and giants loomed
on the wall, swaying to and fro.

Diego didn't
think he
would *ever*
get to sleep.

Diego hid under the covers, hugging his teddy tightly. Then he began to think of Theo, Rosie, and Manish. They'd all been scared of something, like he was now.

If he could help them feel better,
couldn't he help himself feel better, too? Taking a
deep breath, Diego grabbed the flashlight on his
bedside table and shone it bravely under the bed.
All he saw was a pile of board games. There
wasn't a single monster.

Next, he pulled back the curtains and saw
a tall tree swaying in the wind.
It was making the
shadows on Diego's
wall, not ogres
and giants.

Diego smiled and switched off his flashlight.
Now that he knew there was nothing
to be scared of, maybe
he would go to sleep after all.

NOTES FOR PARENTS AND TEACHERS

The aim of this book is to help children think about their feelings in an enjoyable, interactive way. Encourage kids to have fun pointing out details in the illustrations, making sound effects, and role playing. Here are more ideas for getting the most out of the book:

★ Encourage children to talk about their own feelings, if they feel comfortable doing so, either while you are reading the book or afterward. Here are some conversation prompts to try:

  • When are some times you feel scared? Why?

  • How do you stop feeling scared at those times?

  • Why do you think different things scare different people?

  • This story talks about lots of things that people may feel scared about, such as storms, unfamiliar animals, or having to give speeches. What other reasons can you think of?

★ Have children make face masks showing scared expressions. Ask them to explain how these faces show fear.

★ Put on a feelings play! Ask groups of children to act out the different scenarios in the book.

The children could use their face masks to show when they are scared in the play.

★ Have kids make colorful word clouds. They can start by writing the word *scared*, then add any related words they think of, such as *fear* or *nervous*. Have children write their words using different colored pens, making the most important words the biggest and less important words smaller.

★ Ask kids to think of times when they were brave in situations that were scary for them. How did it feel to be brave? Now have them draw pictures or write stories about that time.

★ "HELP! EEK! ARGH!" Words and sounds like these can show that someone is scared. How many more can kids think of? Can they invent any new ones?

★ Invite children to talk about the physical sensations that being scared can bring, and where in their bodies they feel fear. Then discuss things we can do when we feel afraid, such as talking to someone about how we feel, or taking deep breaths to help us feel calmer.

For even more ideas to use with this series, download the free Everyday Feelings Leader's Guide at www.freespirit.com/leader.

Note: If a child is continually fearful or acts out often due to fear or anxiety, seek help from a counselor, psychologist, or other health specialist.

BOOKS TO SHARE

A Book of Feelings by Amanda McCardie, illustrated by
Salvatore Rubbino (Walker, 2016)

F Is for Feelings by Goldie Millar and Lisa A. Berger,
illustrated by Hazel Mitchell (Free Spirit Publishing, 2014)

The Great Big Book of Feelings by Mary Hoffman,
illustrated by Ros Asquith (Frances Lincoln, 2013)

Scaredy Squirrel by Mélanie Watt (Kids Can Press, 2008)

When I Feel Scared by Cornelia Maude Spelman,
illustrated by Kathy Parkinson
(Albert Whitman & Company, 2002)

Who Feels Scared? by Sue Graves,
illustrated by Desideria Guicciardini
(Free Spirit Publishing, 2011)